Little Red Hen's Great Escape

Written by Elizabeth Dale

Illustrated by Andrew Painter

Crabtree Publishing Company

www.crabtreebooks.com

Crabtree Publishing Company

www.crabtreebooks.com
1-800-387-7650

PMB 59051,
350 Fifth Ave., 59th Floor
New York, NY 10118

616 Welland Ave.
St. Catharines, ON
L2M 5V6

Published by Crabtree Publishing in 2016

Series editor: Melanie Palmer
Series designer: Peter Scoulding
Cover designer: Cathryn Gilbert
Series advisor: Catherine Glavina
Editor: Petrice Custance
Notes to adults: Reagan Miller
Prepress technician: Ken Wright
Print production coordinator: Margaret Amy Salter

Text © Elizabeth Dale 2015
Illustration © Andrew Painter 2015

Printed in Canada/012016/BF20151123

First published in
2015 by Franklin Watts
(A division of Hachette
Children's Books)

Library and Archives Canada
Cataloguing in Publication

Dale, Elizabeth, 1952-, author
    Little Red Hen's great escape / Elizabeth Dale ;
illustrated by Andrew Painter.

(Tadpoles fairytale twists)
Issued in print and electronic formats.
ISBN 978-0-7787-2461-2 (bound).--
ISBN 978-0-7787-2512-1 (paperback).--
ISBN 978-1-4271-7721-6 (html)

    I. Painter, Andrew, illustrator II. Title. III.
Series: Tadpoles. Fairytale twists

PZ7.D1523Li 2016   j823'.914   C2015-907111-9
                                     C2015-907112-7

Library of Congress
Cataloging-in-Publication Data

CIP available at Library of Congress

This story is based on the traditional fairy tale,
The Little Red Hen, but with a new twist.
Can you make up your own twist for the story?

The Little Red Hen was worried. Bulldozers had arrived in the farmyard. Holes were being dug. Something bad was going on.

She went to see Farmer Green. She knew he wouldn't tell her what was happening, so she had to be clever.

"The builders are so busy,"

she clucked. "Can I help?"

"You!" laughed the farmer.

"How can you help?"

5

"I can pick up sand and straw to keep it tidy everywhere," the Little Red Hen said.

"OK," said the farmer.
"Be helpful while you can."
The Little Red Hen trembled
with fear. What did he mean?

"Something terrible is happening," she told the pig, the lamb, and the duck. "Please help me find out what it is!"

"Not until eleven o'cluck!"

snorted the pig.

"No, thank ewe,"

laughed the lamb.

"You're just chicken!"
quacked the duck.

"Lazy animals!" thought the
Little Red Hen.

"Something terrible's happening," she told the chickens. "Please help me find out what it is."

"What are you, the Little Head Hen?" clucked one.

"No," said the Little Red Hen.

"But I think we're in danger.

No one else will help me."

The poor Little Red Hen looked
so worried.

"OK!" said the chickens.

"Excellent!" clucked the Little Red
Hen. "Keep your beaks to the
ground, your eyes wide open,
and report back."

So the chickens scurried all over
the farmyard, beaks to the ground,
and eyes wide open.
So did the chicks.

16

Trying not to look suspicious, some chickens pecked at the ground and some hopped around the farm. The Little Red Hen tried to read the workers' plans.

They all met back in the barn.

"There are piles of bricks!" clucked one chick.

"Steel doors!" said another.

"Big walls!" said a third.

"They're planning to keep every animal cooped up inside!" cried the Little Red Hen. "We must tell the others!"

19

"You need some oinkment!" snorted the pig.

"You're utterly quackers!" quacked the duck.

"You're maaaad!" bleated the lamb.

"Well, all the chickens are
leaving!" said the Little Red Hen.
And they did.

The next day, the farmer came
to fetch all the animals.
"Come for a lovely walk,"
he told them.

"Isn't he nice," said the pig, the lamb, and the duck. "The Little Red Hen was just being silly!"

"In you go," smiled the farmer,
opening up a door.

24

"Help!" cried the pig, the lamb, and the duck.

The chickens suddenly appeared
and pushed the farmer inside!
Clunk! went the door.
Click! went the key.

"Hooray!" cried the pig, the lamb, and the duck, making faces at the farmer.

To celebrate their escape, the animals had a wonderful party.

"Everyone, please help clean up!" said the Little Red Hen. All the animals did—after all, they'd learned their lesson.

Puzzle 1

Put these pictures in the correct order. Which
event do you think is the most important?
Now try writing the story in your own words!

Puzzle 2

1. I have got a surprise for the animals!

2. I have found a secret plan.

3. We work well as a team.

4. There is a lot of work to do.

5. We have been spying.

6. Something isn't right on the farm.

Choose the correct speech bubbles for each character. Can you think of any others? Turn the page to find the answers for both puzzles.

Notes for Adults

TADPOLES: Fairytale Twists are engaging, imaginative stories designed for early fluent readers. The books may also be used for read-alouds or shared reading with young children.

TADPOLES: Fairytale Twists are humorous stories with a unique twist on traditional fairy tales. Each story can be compared to the original fairy tale, or appreciated on its own. Fairy tales are a key type of literary text found in the Common Core State Standards.

The following PROMPTS before, during, and after reading support literacy skill development and can enrich shared reading experiences:

1. **Before Reading:** Do a picture walk through the book, previewing the illustrations. Ask the reader to predict what will happen in the story. For example, ask the reader what he or she thinks the twist in the story will be.

2. **During Reading:** Encourage the reader to use context clues and illustrations to determine the meaning of unknown words or phrases.

3. **During Reading:** Have the reader stop midway through the book to revisit his or her predictions. Does the reader wish to change his or her predictions based on what they have read so far?

4. **During and After Reading:** Encourage the reader to make different connections:

   Text-to-Text: How is this story similar to/different from other stories you have read?

   Text-to-World: How are events in this story similar to/different from things that happen in the real world?

   Text-to-Self: Does a character or event in this story remind you of anything in your own life?

5. **After Reading:** Encourage the child to reread the story and to retell it using his or her own words. Invite the child to use the illustrations as a guide.

Here are other titles from TADPOLES: Fairytale Twists for you to enjoy:

Answers

Puzzle 1
The correct order is: 1c, 2f, 3e, 4a, 5b, 6d
Puzzle 2
The Little Red Hen: 2, 6
The farmer: 1, 4   The chicks: 3, 5